Bulbasaur's Bad Day

Pokémon junior

#4

There are more books about Pokémon for younger readers.

COLLECT THEM ALL!

#1 Surf's Up, Pikachu!

#2 Meowth, the Big Mouth

#3 Save Our Squirtle!

#4 Bulbasaur's Bad Day

COMING SOON!

#5 Two of a Kind

Bulbasaur's Bad Day

POKÉMON junior

#4

By Bill Michaels

SCHOLASTIC INC.
New York Toronto London Auckland Sydney
Mexico City New Delhi Hong Kong

If you purchased this book without a cover, you should be aware that this book is stolen property. It was reported as "unsold and destroyed" to the publisher, and neither the author nor the publisher has received any payment for this "stripped book."

No part of this publication may be reproduced in whole or in part, or stored in a retrieval system, or transmitted in any form or by any means, electronic, mechanical, photocopying, recording, or otherwise, without written permission of the publisher. For information regarding permission, write to Scholastic Inc., Attention: Permissions Department, 555 Broadway, New York, NY 10012.

ISBN 0-439-15427-8

© 1995, 1996, 1998 Nintendo, CREATURES, GAME FREAK.
TM and ® are trademarks of Nintendo.
© 2000 Nintendo.

Published by Scholastic Inc. All rights reserved.
SCHOLASTIC and associated logos are trademarks
and/or registered trademarks of Scholastic Inc.

Designed by Joan Moloney

12 11 10 9 8 7 6 5 4 3 2 1   0 1 2 3 4 5 6/0

Printed in the U.S.A.
First Scholastic printing, June 2000

CHAPTER ONE

One Grumpy Pokémon

"*Bulba. Bulbasaur.*" Bulbasaur was in a grumpy mood. It was saying, *This rain better stop soon.*

It had been raining for five days in Celadon City. Bulbasaur, Pikachu, Togepi, and Squirtle were stuck inside at the Trainers'

Hostel. Ash, Misty, and Tracey were there, too. So was Tracey's Pokémon, Marill. The friends were on their journey to become the world's greatest Pokémon trainers. Usually, they had fun. But now, no one was having a good time. Bulbasaur was the most cranky of all.

"Bulbasaur. Bulba-bulba-saur?" *Can't we get out of this place?*

"Squirtle. Squirtle-squirtle," said Squirtle.

It looks like the rain is stop-ping.

The five Pokémon looked out the window. The rain had stopped! Now their trainers would take them outside for sure!

Just then, Ash walked in with Misty and Tracey. "Bad news, guys," Ash said to the Pokémon. "My Pokédex is broken. I have to get Professor Oak to fix it."

"*Pikachu*?" asked Pikachu. *Are we all going?*

"No, Professor Oak says it is safer for you to stay here," said

Ash. "Team Rocket will not be able to steal you from a Trainers' Hostel."

"*Pika*," said Pikachu. Pikachu was disappointed, but it knew that Ash was right.

"Only Togepi will go with us," said Misty. Togepi was too little to be away from Misty for long.

"Professor Oak says it will not take long. Will you guys be all right without us for one night?" Ash asked.

"*Pika pika*," said Pikachu. *Yes, Ash. We will be fine.*

"*Marill mar?*" asked Marill. *Can we go out now that the rain has stopped?*

"You guys can go to the Celadon City Gym tonight," Tracey said. "But be careful. And come home right away. Another storm is coming."

Ash said good-bye to all the Pokémon. Then he gave Pikachu a big hug. "Take care of yourself, Pikachu. See you tomorrow!"

"*Pikachu!*" said Pikachu. *Good-bye!*

CHAPTER TWO

Fun at the Gym

As soon as the trainers were gone, Squirtle stood up on its hind legs. "*Squirtle!*" *We are on our own!*

"*Bulba! Bulba,*" said Bulbasaur. *Yes! It is just us.*

"*Pika. Pikachu!*" said Pikachu. *Come on, everyone. To the gym!*

The four Pokémon were excited. They would miss their trainers, but they would have fun on their own. They headed over to the Celadon City Gym.

Bulbasaur and Squirtle joked with each other on the way. Squirtle used its Tail Whip to touch Bulbasaur's nose. Bulbasaur used its Vine Whip to scratch Squirtle's head. Everyone laughed.

At the gym, two Pokémon were having a contest. It was

Butterfree and Articuno!

Bulbasaur pointed. "*Bulba!*"
Look!

Articuno was a very rare
Pokémon! Hardly anyone ever
saw it! This was amazing!

The gym was filled with
Pokémon and their trainers.
Everyone was cheering.

The beautiful blue Articuno
was flying high in the air.
Butterfree was flying, too, but it
was staying low. It was waiting for
Articuno to fly closer. Articuno
pretended it was flying higher.

But it was only a trick! Suddenly, it flew down very fast. It was going to use its Ice Beam!

But Butterfree was ready. It was very calm. Articuno came very close.

"Pikachu!"

Pikachu was so excited it grabbed Bulbasaur's bulb. *Watch out, Butterfree!*

CHAPTER THREE

A Good Joke

Butterfree remained calm. It waited until Articuno was very close. Then it flapped its wings as fast as it could. It was going to use its Sleep Powder! *Poof!*

Articuno flew right into the powder! It fell asleep instantly. Down, down, down it glided. It

landed softly on the floor of the gym. Butterfree had won!

The crowd went wild.

Marill could not believe it. *"Marill! Marill!" What a great contest! Butterfree was so brave!*

Psyduck came up to the group. It was laughing.

Marill was curious. *"Marill?" What is so funny? Tell us!*

"Psy-aye." I heard a joke. It is making me laugh.

"Bulba!" Tell us!

"Psy. Psyduck. Psy." It is a riddle. What is supposed to be very fast — but never gets anywhere?

The four Pokémon looked at one another. They did not know the answer.

Psyduck laughed. *"Psyduck. Psy-aye-aye."* The answer is TEAM ROCKET!

"Bul-bul-bul-bul-bul." Bulbasaur could not stop laughing.

"*Pi-pi-pi-pi-pi.*" Pikachu was laughing, too.

"*Squirtle.*" Squirtle scratched its head. *I don't get it.*

The four Pokémon said good-bye to Psyduck. They left the gym. When they were outside, Pikachu explained the joke to Squirtle. Squirtle threw up its hands and laughed.

They were walking back to the hostel when Bulbasaur stopped.

"*Bulba!*" *Stop! I have an idea!*

"*Marill?*" *What is it?*

CHAPTER FOUR

Bulbasaur Has an Idea

"*Bul-bulba-bulbasaur.*" *We can take a shortcut home. We could go through the forest.*

"*Pika?*" *A shortcut?*

"*Bulbasaur!*" *Yes! Rattata told me about it.*

Marill was excited. "*Marill!*" *We will get home much faster!*

"Bulba." Much, much faster. Remember Ash said to come home quickly.

Only Pikachu was a little nervous.

"Pika? Pika pi?" Should we? Without our trainers?

"Bulba bulbasaur!" Of course we should! And maybe we will spot a wild Mankey in the forest!

Pikachu thought that would be fun. But it was still not sure.

"*Pika?*" *Are you sure you know the way?*

Bulbasaur laughed. "*Bulbasaur!*" *I am very sure. Come on!*

Pikachu thought about seeing a wild Mankey. And it thought about getting home sooner. "*Pika!*" *Okay!*

So the four Pokémon set off for the forest. Bulbasaur was leading the way.

They were happy. They would find their way home. And they would do it without Ash, Tracey, and Misty! Their trainers would be proud.

Off they went. Pretty soon, they could see the forest. It was late in the afternoon. The sun was starting to set. But the four Pokémon did not notice. They were much too excited.

Marill pointed. *Look! Weedle!*

It was true! They could see Weedle eating some leaves. It was just at the edge of the forest. Marill, Squirtle, and Pikachu watched. They did not notice that Bulbasaur was walking straight into the forest!

"Marill?" Where are you

going,
Bulbasaur?

Bulbasaur looked
back. *"Bulbasaur."*
I am going to the shortcut.
Come on!

"Pika! Pika!" *Wait for us!*

But Bulbasaur did not hear
Pikachu. It walked into the forest.
The other Pokémon hurried to
catch up.

CHAPTER FIVE

Trouble

Squirtle was very upset.

"Squirtle! Squirtle!" Bulbasaur! *You slow down!*

Bulbasaur was scratching its head. *"Bulba."* Let me see. Was it *this way? Or that way?*

"Pika?" You mean you do not know the way?

"*Bulba. Bulba,*" Well, yes. Of course I do . . . I think.

"*Pika?*" Which way is it?

Bulbasaur looked one way. Then it looked another way.

"*Bulbasaur!*" This way. Follow me!

Bulbasaur took a step forward. Then it disappeared!

Squirtle, Marill, and Pikachu looked at one another. What had happened?

They walked over to where Bulbasaur had vanished. There was a big pit! It was deep and

wide. And inside the pit was Bulbasaur! It had fallen in!

It was a trap! Who could have done this? It must have been — Meowth! Who else  would do such a mean thing?

"Pika?" Are you all right, Bulbasaur?

"Bulba! Bulba bulbasaur." I am fine. I was not looking. I fell in. Now, here I am! Bulbasaur did

not seem too upset.

"*Squirtle squirtle.*" *Do not worry. We will get you out.*

"*Bulba bulbasaur.*" *I can get out by myself. I will use my Vine Whip.*

Then they all heard something. It was the rumble of thunder.

Pikachu looked up at the sky. "*Pika pika.*" *Tracey said there would be a storm. Here it is!*

"*Squirtle.*" *Well, we have to do something. Fast!*

Just then, it started to rain!

CHAPTER SIX

Things Get Worse

Pikachu felt the raindrops hit its head. It started to rain very hard. Pretty soon, it was pouring.

Bulbasaur looked up from the pit. It looked sad. *"Bulba bulbasaur." I was wrong. I cannot get out by myself!*

Squirtle leaned over.

"*Squirtle!*" *Do not worry. We will help you. But we have to hurry.*

Marill knew exactly what Squirtle meant. "*Marill. Marill,*" *We must work fast. We have to get you out before the pit fills up with water!*

Squirtle tried to use its Bubble Attack. It wanted to slow down the rain. But it was no use. The rain was coming down too fast.

"Pika!" Someone has to go back to the hostel for help!

"Squirtle squirt." I will go! I will find help.

Now, it was just Marill, Pikachu, and poor Bulbasaur.

Then, all of the sudden . . .

"Meowth," said a familiar voice. "What have we here?"

Out from the forest stepped Meowth. It was grinning. It walked over to the pit and looked down at Bulbasaur.

"My, my," Meowth said. "Look who decided to drop in."

CHAPTER SEVEN

Bulbasaur Fights Back

Bulbasaur looked up at Meowth. *"Bulba bulba!" So, it is you!*

"You were expecting maybe Santa Claus?" said Meowth.

"Bulba!" When I get out of here . . .

"You do not look like you are

going anywhere." Meowth
laughed.

Just then,
Gastly and
Arbok appeared.
Arbok wiggled
over to Meowth.
It looked at
Bulbasaur in the pit.

"*Arbok*," it said. *Look at that
foolish Pokémon.*

Bulbasaur became angry. It was
mad at itself for going into the
forest without the trainers. And it
was angry at Meowth and Arbok

for making fun of it.

"Bulbaaaa!" You will be sorry! Suddenly, Bulbasaur unleashed its Leech Seed. Gastly and Arbok fought back. Arbok used its Poison Sting. Gastly tried to use its Night Shade.

Pikachu and Marill were scared. Pikachu tried its Thundershock, but it was raining too hard. The lightning was flashing. The thunder was booming. And inch by inch the pit was

filling up with water. How much longer could Bulbasaur last?

"*Pika?*" said Pikachu. *Where is Squirtle?*

Meowth laughed. "Squirtle? It probably buried itself under some leaves!"

Suddenly, Marill heard something. It could hear better than any other Pokémon. It could hear sounds from far, far away.

"*Marill!*" *Someone is coming! It is Squirtle!*

"*Pikachu!*" *I cannot hear a thing!*

"Marill!" *I can hear Squirtle's footsteps. Do not be afraid, Bulbasaur. I know Squirtle is coming soon!*

Bulbasaur suddenly felt a little better. The water was getting higher. But Bulbasaur was brave. Suddenly, someone burst into clearing.

"Squirtle! Squirtle!" Do not be afraid! I have brought help!

But what help did Squirtle bring? It was alone.

Just then, there was a flash in the sky.

"Ah, just some more lightning," said Meowth. "Get on with the show. We are going to bring you back to Team Rocket."

Then everyone heard a loud growl. There was another flash. They looked up in the sky.

It was Charizard! It was flying in the sky. It was spitting fire. And it was very, very angry.

CHAPTER EIGHT

Is It Too Late?

Charizard!

Even Meowth looked scared!

Suddenly, everything changed.

Charizard used its Rage and

Growl. Then it used its mighty

Flamethrower. Gastly and Arbok

began inching away. Meowth

looked scared.

Bulbasaur took heart. It pulled out its Razor Leaf. Watch out! Pikachu joined in with a Thunder Wave. Suddenly, the battle was changing. Bulbasaur and its friends were winning!

Gastly and Arbok ran away into the forest. Meowth turned to run, too. But first it said, "Big deal. You are still in deep trouble,

Bulbasaur. And I mean *deep!*"
Meowth laughed and disappeared
into the forest.

It was true. Bulbasaur was still
in the pit. The storm
was still raging.
What could
Bulbasaur do?
The water was almost up
to Bulbasaur's neck. *"Bulba!" I
am tired. I am afraid!*

*"Pika! Pika!" Your friends are
here! We will never leave you!*

"Squirtle!" We will rescue

you! We will think of a way. Hold on!

Squirtle, Marill, and Pikachu formed a little circle. How could they rescue Bulbasaur? Each Pokémon had an idea. They worked together. In a short time, they had a plan!

Pikachu went to the edge of the pit. It spoke to Bulbasaur. *"Pikachu. Pika." I will use the power of the storm.*

"Marill." The storm will help us, not hurt us. Just watch.

CHAPTER TEN

Pikachu to the Rescue

Pikachu stepped back. It looked up into the sky. It waited.

Suddenly, there was a lightning bolt. Pikachu used its Thunder Shock. It used its Agility to guide the Thunder Shock. It made the lightning hit a tree!

Down came the tree. It fell

right into Bulbasaur's pit. It leaned up from the bottom like a slide. Bulbasaur could climb out! It would use the tree as a ladder.

But what was this? A group of wild Mankeys! They were in the tree! They ran down the tree into the pit.

Marill looked worried. *"Marill."*

This might be trouble. They look angry.

"Squirt squirtle." Well, at least we have seen a Mankey.

But the Mankeys were not angry at all! They all ran down the tree and helped pull Bulbasaur out of the pit.

Bulbasaur ran over to its friends. They all hugged. They were happy.

The wild Mankeys waved and ran off into the forest.

"Pika, pika!" Pikachu waved back at the Mankeys. *Thank you!*

Bulbasaur looked very sad. *"Bulba bulbasaur." I am sorry. I got us all in trouble. I did not know the way. I just wanted to sound like I knew what I was doing.*

Pikachu hugged Bulbasaur.

"Pikachu!" That is all right. Do not feel bad. It is not your fault.

And now we are safe because we helped one another.

"Squirtle!" Time to go home! I

really do know the way now!

It was dark now. But Squirtle guided the Pokémon.

They were all very tired. What a day! They had had many adventures. Too many!

Finally, they reached the edge of the forest. Bulbasaur looked back. It shivered a little. It would never go in there again without Ash!

The Pokémon finally got back to the hostel. They were all tired out. Soon they were sound asleep.

CHAPTER TEN

The Trainers Return

The next morning, Bulbasaur, Squirtle, Pikachu, and Marill felt much better. They had all slept well. The day before seemed like a nightmare. They could hardly believe it had all happened.

Outside, the day was cool and clear. The sun was shining.

45

Pikachu scratched its head. *"Pika?" Did we really do all those things yesterday?*

"Marill." I think so.

Bulbasaur remembered everything too well. *"Bulba." I know so!*

"Squirtle squirt," said Squirtle. *Me too!*

Then they saw Ash, Misty, and Tracey. They had returned from their trip. The Pokémon were very happy to see their trainers! They ran over to Ash, Misty, and Tracey and hugged them.

"Hello," said Ash. "Is everything okay?"

"Bulba bulbasaur!" Sure. But *being without you — well, it is the pits!*

Pikachu and Meowth . . . friends forever?!

POKéMON junior™

Chapter Book #5:
Two of a Kind

It's no secret that the evil Team Rocket is out to get Pikachu. But when they kidnap Squirtle to get to the little lightning mouse, they've gone too far! Can Pikachu and pals save their friend in time? Or will the tiny turtle become Team Rocket's newest member?

Visit us at www.scholastic.com

©1995, 1996, 1998 Nintendo. CREATURES, GAME FREAK, TM & ® are trademarks of Nintendo. © 2000 Nintendo.

◣SCHOLASTIC

POKJR999